Dear Parent:
Your child's love of reading starts here!

Every child learns to read in a different way and at his or her own speed. Some go back and forth between reading levels and read favorite books again and again. Others read through each level in order. You can help your young reader improve and become more confident by encouraging his or her own interests and abilities. From books your child reads with you to the first books he or she reads alone, there are I Can Read Books for every stage of reading:

SHARED READING
Basic language, word repetition, and whimsical illustrations, ideal for sharing with your emergent reader

BEGINNING READING
Short sentences, familiar words, and simple concepts for children eager to read on their own

READING WITH HELP
Engaging stories, longer sentences, and language play for developing readers

READING ALONE
Complex plots, challenging vocabulary, and high-interest topics for the independent reader

ADVANCED READING
Short paragraphs, chapters, and exciting themes for the perfect bridge to chapter books

I Can Read Books have introduced children to the joy of reading since 1957. Featuring award-winning authors and illustrators and a fabulous cast of beloved characters, I Can Read Books set the standard for beginning readers.

A lifetime of discovery begins with the magical words "I Can Read!"

Visit www.icanread.com for information
on enriching your child's reading experience.

I Can Read Book® is a trademark of HarperCollins Publishers.

Library of Congress Cataloging-in-Publication Data is available.
ISBN 978-0-06-185384-5 (trade bdg.) — ISBN 978-0-06-185383-8 (pbk.)

09 10 11 12 13 LP/WOR 10 9 8 7 6 5 4 3 2 1 ❖ First Edition

I Can Read!

READING 2 WITH HELP

BIG ADVENTURE

**BASED ON THE BESTSELLING BOOKS
BY JOHN GROGAN**

COVER ILLUSTRATION BY RICHARD COWDREY

BY SUSAN HILL

**INTERIOR ILLUSTRATIONS BY
LYDIA HALVERSON**

HARPER

An Imprint of HarperCollinsPublishers

4

Marley woke up his family
one morning
with a "ruff-ruff-ruff!"
"Bad dog, Marley," said Daddy.
"It's too soon to wake up."

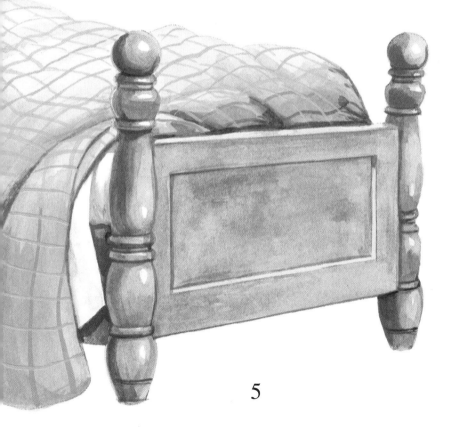

Cassie and Baby Louie
were ready to play.
Cassie jumped out of bed.
But Baby Louie couldn't get out
of his crib.

Marley stared at the crib.

"I'll get you out of that cage!"

he thought.

Marley jumped into the crib.

Then he hung Baby Louie over the rail.

"Bad dog, Marley!" yelled Mommy.

"Baby Louie could get hurt!"

Daddy made breakfast.

He flipped a pancake.

Up flew the pancake.

Up jumped Marley.

He fetched the pancake in midair.

"Bad dog, Marley!" yelled Daddy.

"Run and get dressed
so we can go to the playground,"
Mommy said to Cassie.

Marley ran to the kids' room.

He pulled all the clothes

from all the drawers.

"Bad dog, Marley!" yelled Cassie.

Mommy put Marley outside.

"We need a break," she said.

Marley howled.

It was a sad sound.

"Maybe they don't love me now,"

he thought.

Marley began to dig.

He dug until he could slip

under the fence.

Then Marley ran away!

He ran past the school,

the library, and the park.

He ran far away from everything

and everyone he loved.

After a while,

Cassie went to get Marley.

"Oh, no!" she cried.

"Marley is gone!"

"Why did he run away?" asked Cassie.

"Doesn't he know we love him?"

Mommy hugged Cassie.

"We'll find him," she said.

"We'll tell him we love him."

Marley was still running.

He missed his family.

His paws hurt from digging.

Suddenly, a wonderful smell

stopped Marley in his tracks.

It smelled better than dog chow,

better than a bone,

better than Baby Louie's sticky face.

"Well, hello there,"

said the man inside the shop.

"Welcome to my bakery."

Marley licked the baker's face all over.

"My new home!" he thought.

The baker laughed.

"Good dog," he said.

"I had a dog like you once."

The baker saw Marley's dog tag.

He knew this dog had run away.

"I'll call your owners as soon as

I take these cookies

out of the oven," said the baker.

"Be a good dog and
guard the cookies,"
the baker said to Marley.
Then he went to call
Marley's family.

Marley stared at the cookies.

He sniffed at the cakes.

Everything smelled so good!

He started sniffing everything.

Marley sniffed a bag of flour.

Achoo! Marley sneezed.

He jumped and bumped into the table.

Flour, cakes, and cookies

went everywhere.

Then the baker came back.

"My cookies! My cakes!"

yelled the baker.

"And there was no answer

at your house!"

Marley gently set a cookie
at the baker's feet.

The baker scratched Marley's ears.

"You didn't mean to make a mess,"
he said kindly.

Just then, Marley's family ran by.

They'd looked all over for Marley.

"Look at that mess!" said Mommy.

Suddenly, they all stopped.

They knew what that meant.

"Marley!" they shouted.

Mommy, Daddy, Cassie,
and Baby Louie ran inside the bakery
and found their dog at last.
"We love you even if we yell,"
Mommy said.

"We love you even if you
make a mess of our house,"
said Daddy.
"And of my bakery!" said the baker.

Everyone helped the baker clean up.

Marley wagged his tail so hard

he knocked over a chair.

He wanted to help, too.

"Look!" cried Cassie.
"Marley's cleaning up all
the broken cookies!"

"Ruff-ruff-ruff!"

"I know what that means,"

said Cassie.

"And we love you, too, Marley!"